This Book Belongs to...

Name:

Age:

To my daughter, Isobel.

I will always remember this day, when we walked home from nursery and you created an imaginary dragon adventure with Hagley. This will always be one of my most treasured memories.

Written By Clare Beckett
Illustrated By Adam Walker-Parker
Edited By Danielle Wilkins

Published in association with Bear With Us Productions

The adventures of

Isobel & HAGLEY

The Dragon Adventure

Written By Clare Beckett

Illustrated By Adam Walker-Parker

BEAR W!TH US PRODUCTIONS

It was 3pm and Isobel
had finished school.

Outside, her mum and Hagley
were waiting for her.

As they walked home, Isobel picked up a stick from the floor. "En garde!" Isobel laughed, as she pointed the stick at Hagley

Hagley picked up his own stick in self-defence.

At that moment, a squirrel scurried down the tree in front of them, making them both jump!

"I thought it was a dragon," laughed Isobel.

And with a cheeky wink and a
click of his fingers, suddenly
Hagley was dressed as a knight
in his shining armour.

Isobel's book bag and stick
had turned into a shield
and a sword.

As they marched along the path towards home, a dragon appeared from nowhere, running into the bushes.

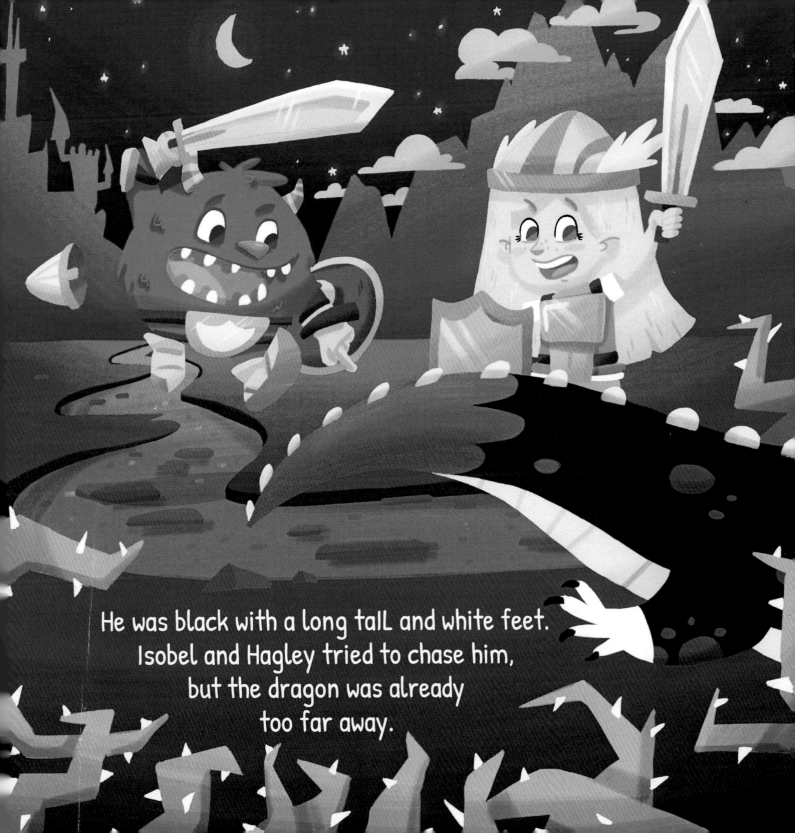

He was black with a long talL and white feet.
Isobel and Hagley tried to chase him,
but the dragon was already
too far away.

As they crept along a little further, Isobel and Hagley could hear a rustling in the grass.

"Charrrrrrrge!"

Isobel roared, as she and Hagley ran into the long grass, swinging their swords.

Suddenly, up flew a tiny dragon with a red belly. He had been hiding beneath the tree.

The pair carried on
their journey
towards home...

...when suddenly they came upon a loud, flowing river.
Isobel and Hagley needed to cross the river to
get to the other side.

As they held hands and prepared to step into the water,
a river dragon went zooming past.

"Phew!" said Isobel.
"That was close!"
Suddenly Isobel spotted a bridge
that would allow them to cross.

As Isobel and Hagley got closer to the gates of home...

...They could see
it was being guarded
by a huge green dragon.

They crept along the pathway
and hid behind the brick wall.
"We need to come up with a plan,"
whispered Isobel.

Hagley put up this shield and sword, and jumped
out from behind the wall, Startling the dragon.
As the dragon leapt up in the air,
Isobel ran between his legs,
heading straight for the gates.

With a wave of his sword
and shield to protect him
from the dragon's fiery flame...

Hagley ran for the gates,
slipping through the gap
just in time.

The dragon sloped off grumpily
back to his cave.

With the front door closed and Isobel and Hagley safely inside, Hagley clicked his fingers and their dragon adventure was over.

At bedtime, the pair both fell about laughing,
as Hagley made shadow dragons on the wall.

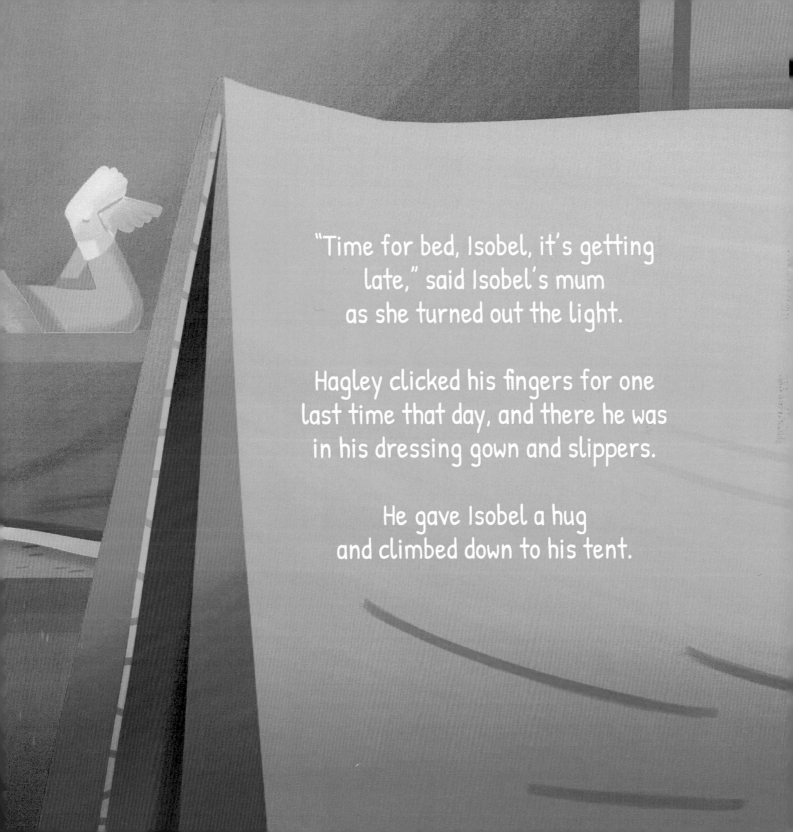

"Time for bed, Isobel, it's getting
late," said Isobel's mum
as she turned out the light.

Hagley clicked his fingers for one
last time that day, and there he was
in his dressing gown and slippers.

He gave Isobel a hug
and climbed down to his tent.

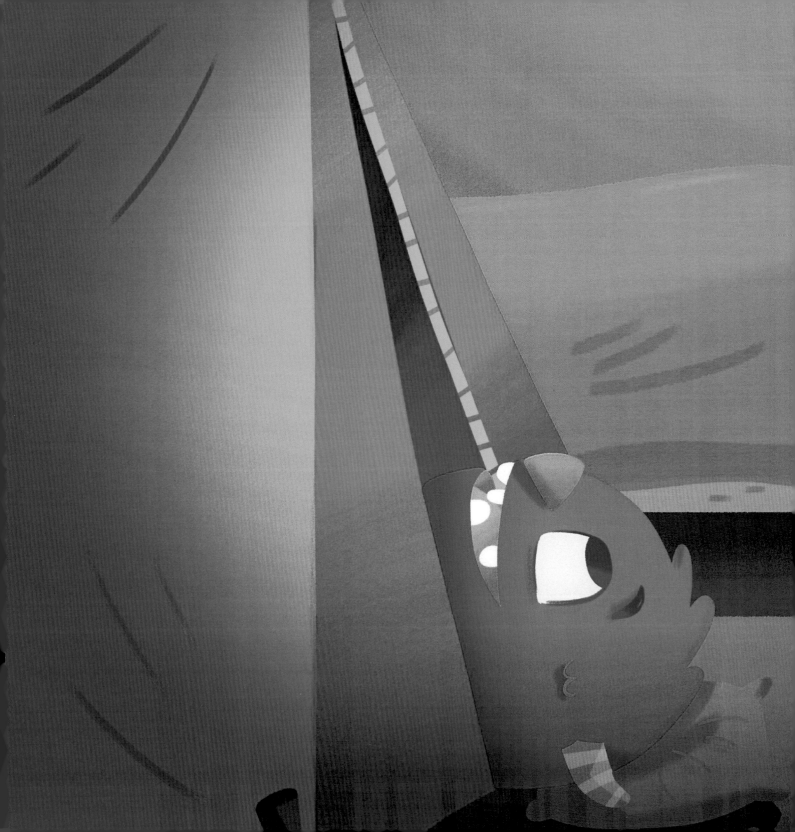

"Goodnight, Isobel," Hagley said.
"Goodnight Hagley," whispered Isobel,
still smiling about her and Hagley's dragon adventure.

The
End

Join Isobel & HAGLEY

On another exciting adventure!

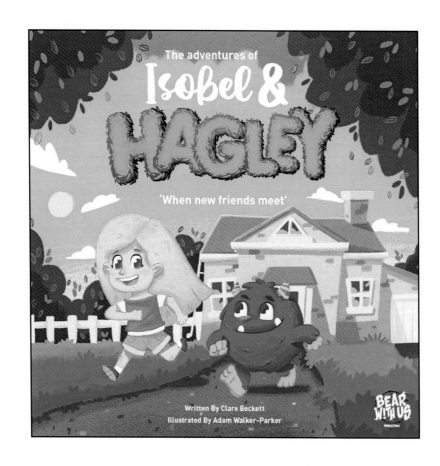

Join the
Dots!